Vol. 2 Chapter 1:
the broken truth,

MISS VESPER GREY?

IS THAT YOU?!

HELLO, FREDERICK.

I HAVEN'T SEEN YOU SINCE YOU WERE JUST A LITTLE THING.

IT'S BEEN TOO LONG.

IT HAS.

THIS IS CORRICK.

GREETINGS, YOUNG MAN.

HMPH.

SO, WHAT BRINGS YOU OUT HERE?

I WAS HOPING YOU COULD HOLD A FEW MORE ARTIFACTS FOR SAFEKEEPING.

OF COURSE. I'M ALWAYS HAPPY TO HOARD ANOTHER DANGEROUS, LIFE-THREATENING PIECE OF HISTORY FOR YOU GREYS.

HOW'S YOUR FATHER ANYWAY?

OH.

VESPER?!

VESPER?

IT'S LIKE...

LOSING HER ALL OVER AGAIN.

AND MY FATHER... HE..

LIED TO ME.

DID YOU KNOW?

CORRICK.

DID YOU KNOW MY MOTHER WAS MURDERED?

VESPER...

WHAT ELSE DO YOU KNOW?

THERE ARE THINGS THAT YOU JUST DON'T NEED TO--

BULLSHIT!

MY WHOLE LIFE, I'VE BEEN FED LIES.

I DON'T NEED THEM FROM <u>YOU</u>.

AND WHAT GOOD WOULD COME FROM KNOWING?

I NEED TO KNOW WHAT HAPPENED TO HER.

SHE WAS MY <u>MOTHER</u>!

I WILL NOT FEED YOUR DESIRE FOR VENGEANCE!

FINE.

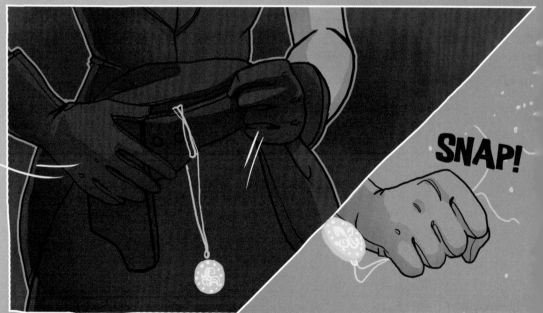

SNAP!

GUH...

THEN I SUPPOSE I DON'T NEED THIS ANYMORE.

I KNOW YOU'RE HURT...

I KNOW YOU NEED TO LASH OUT...

BUT VESPER, DON'T DO THIS.

I CAN'T TAKE ANY MORE LIES, CORRICK...

ESPECIALLY FROM YOU.

SIGH

ALRIGHT...

YOU WANT TO KNOW EVERYTHING?

YES.

FINE. I'LL TELL YOU.

BUT, NOT HERE.

ALRIGHT.

WE'RE HERE.

SO, TALK.

FLOP

MY FATHER'S JOURNAL?

MY MOTHER...

SHE DIED PROTECTING THE AMULET?

SHE DIED PROTECTING HER DAUGHTER.

AND YOU...?

YOU WERE WITH ME ALL THOSE YEARS AGO?

YES.

SEE...

THERE WERE EIGHT PEOPLE THAT DAY MAGNUS FOUND BENNETT.

HE KILLED SEVEN.

THE LONE SURVIVOR WAS A YOUNG MAN...

BENNETT'S SON.

DOMINICK.

WHAT?

ALL THAT TIME, DOMINICK WAS RIGHT UNDER MAGNUS' NOSE.

BIDING HIS TIME.

WHY?

WHAT WAS DOM WAITING FOR?

HE KNEW HE WAS OUTMATCHED.

BY WHO?

MY FATHER?

NO.

BY ME.

WHEN DOMINICK FINALLY CONFRONTED MAGNUS, DOM WAS NEARLY OBLITERATED.

DOM HAD TO GET THE AMULET OUT OF THE WAY.

AND HE KNEW JUST HOW TO DO IT.

HE THREATENED ME, DIDN'T HE?

SO, PAPA GAVE ME BACK THE AMULET.

I REMEMBER...

YOU HAVE TO KEEP THIS ON YOU, AT ALL TIMES.

NEVER LOSE IT, OKAY?

OKAY, PAPA.

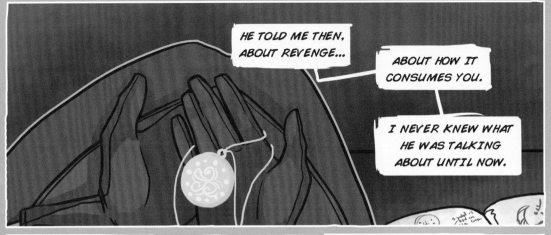

THE MISSING PAGES, CORRICK.

WHAT WERE THEY?!

JOURNAL ENTRIES.

AND YOU TORE THEM OUT?

YOU DESTROYED THEM?

SIGH

NOT ALL OF THEM.

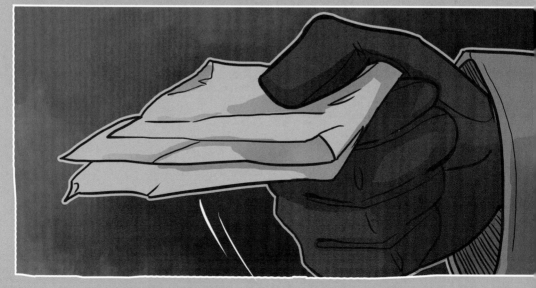

MM.

I DIDN'T WANT YOU GOING AFTER IT.

ALRIGHT?

AFTER WHAT?

SIGH.

THE CITY OF AURU.

MY CITY.

OH.

Vol. 2 Chapter 2:
the city laced with gold

WOW.

HOME SWEET HOME...

EH, CORY?

COMPLETE WITH AN EMBARRASSING FAMILY PORTRAIT.

ALRIGHT, SPREAD OUT!

SEE WHAT YOU CAN FIND.

AND BE CAREFUL!

YOU'RE A WELL-READ SCHOLAR OF HISTORY...

YOU DON'T NEED ME TO TELL YOU.

AND WHO IS THIS GUY?

SIGH.

KING ARICON.

YOU WANTED TO SEE ME, YOUR GRACE?

AH, CORRICK...

MY DEAR BROTHER.

I WAS HOPING TO GLEAN SOME INSIGHT FROM YOU.

OF COURSE.

I'M FEARFUL, BROTHER.

WITH AZEEL'S DEATH, I'VE GROWN SUSPICIOUS OF EVERYONE.

I CAN'T SLEEP, I CAN'T EAT...

I FEAR SOMEONE WILL TRY TO KILL ME TOO.

"TOO"?

WHAT DO YOU MEAN "TOO"?

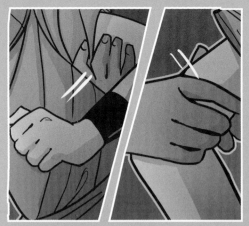

YOU CANNOT HARM ME, BROTHER.

DESPITE YOUR DESIRE TO TRY.

I DID THIS FOR BOTH OF US.

FOR OUR MORTALITY.

FOR OUR CITY.

I'VE GIVEN YOU A GREAT POWER, BROTHER.

YOU SHOULD BE HONORED.

AT THE PRICE OF EVERYTHING.

WHY COULDN'T YOU'VE JUST KILLED ME TOO?

FOR EIGHT YEARS...

I WAS ENSLAVED TO A MAN WHO DESTROYED MY WORLD...

FORCED TO PROTECT HIM FROM HARM...

...WHEN ALL I WANTED TO DO WAS DRIVE A KNIFE THROUGH HIS CHEST.

I SUPPOSE THE DESIRE FOR MURDER RAN IN THE FAMILY.

SO, WHAT HAPPENED AFTER THOSE 8 YEARS?

MY FOOLISH BROTHER...

ALL THAT TIME, WRECKING MYSELF WITH WAYS TO GET VENGENCE...

WHEN ALL I HAD TO DO WAS WAIT FOR ARICON TO DO IT FOR ME.

HE WAS MAD WITH POWER.

USED BLACK MAGIC TO RULE THE CITY.

HE THOUGHT HE WAS PROTECTING IT...

BUT HE'D MERELY DOOMED IT FROM THE START.

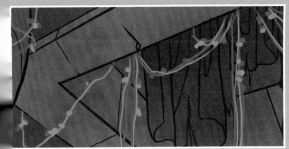

NOW, RUN.

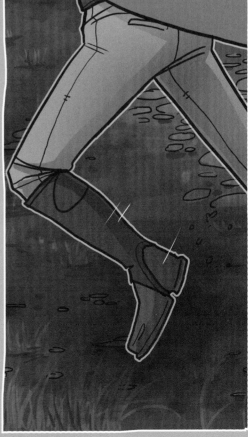

END CHAPTER TWO

Vol. 2 Chapter 3:
closing the distance

HOW'D YOU FIND US?

OH, I WAS A BLOODHOUND IN ANOTHER LIFE.

THAT, AND WHEN A HORSE AND CARRIAGE ZIP BY SPEWING FLAMES...

PEOPLE TEND TO REMEMBER.

WELL, EXCUSE ME FOR SHAVING HALF A DAY OFF OUR TRIP!

WHY DO YOU WANT TO COME, TEGAN?

BECAUSE I MISSED THIS FACE.

SQUISH SQUISH

AND BECAUSE I WANT TO HELP.

IT'LL BE DANGEROUS.

WHAT? I DIDN'T TELL YOU?

'DANGEROUS' IS MY MIDDLE NAME!

•••

WELL... OKAY, IT'S MIRANDA...

BUT, IT'S A LOOSE TRANSLATION.

PLUS, I CAN HELP YOU LOCATE DOM.

AND HOW WILL YOU DO THAT?

HE'S BEEN TAILING ME FOR DAYS.

THE MAN IS PERSISTENT, I'LL GIVE HIM THAT.

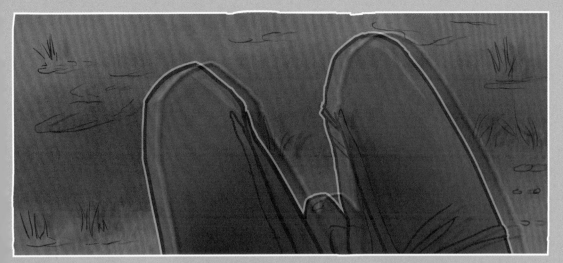

GNGH...

AH!

SIGH

GREAT.

ARE WE GOING TO REMINISCE ABOUT WHO WRONGED WHO NOW?

BECAUSE, FRANKLY, IT'S EXHAUSTING.

VESPER, LEAVE HIM.

Y'KNOW WHAT? I GOT THIS.

POW!

"IT"?

I KNOW WHAT YOU ARE AFTER...

WHAT COULD SEVERELY BENEFIT SUNSHINE OVER THERE.

AND BELIEVE ME, YOU DON'T WANT TO FIND IT.

YOU KNOW WHERE THE BOOK IS...

DON'T YOU?

WELL, THAT DOESN'T SOUND OMINOUS AT ALL.

VESPER, WE CAN'T CONFRONT THIS THING.

IF IT'S THE SAME CREATURE WE CAME ACROSS IN AURU...

YOU'RE SIDING WITH DOM NOW?

THIS IS FOOLISH.

WE'RE GOING.

MY FATHER WARNED ABOUT THIS.

"SOMETHING IS COMING..."

IT MAY HAVE STARTED WITH HIM...

BUT, IT'LL END WITH ME.

CLAK!

?

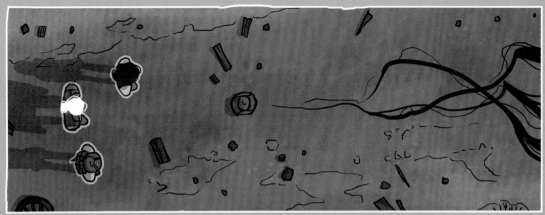

Vol. 2 Chapter 4:
then it comes crashing down

I'M A DARK MISTAKE.

A DEEP REGRET.

I'M THE BAD MEMORY THAT STEALS YOUR SLEEP...

YOU GOT A SHORTER NAME?

AZEEL.

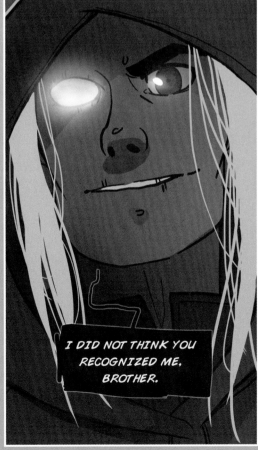

I DID NOT THINK YOU RECOGNIZED ME, BROTHER.

YOUR BROTHER?!

WELL, THAT MAKES SENSE.

ARICON.

HE DESTROYED YOUR LIFE TOO.

HE DESTROYED EVERYTHING THAT STOOD IN HIS WAY.

BUT THAT'S THE BEAUTY OF IT.

IN HIS HASTE, HE MADE US STRONGER.

I WOULDN'T CALL THIS AN IMPROVEMENT.

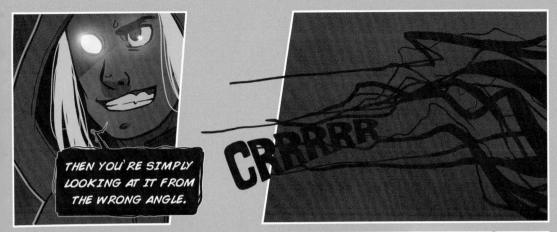

THEN YOU'RE SIMPLY LOOKING AT IT FROM THE WRONG ANGLE.

CRRRRR

AH!

HCK!

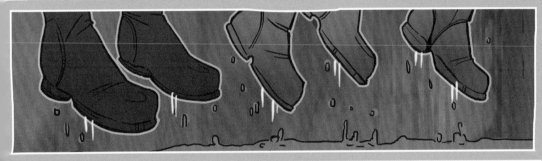

AH!

SHIT.

I DID NOT SIGN UP FOR THIS.

WHAT DID YOU DO TO HIM?!

WHERE IS HE?

YOUR FATHER REALLY DID KNOW HOW TO STEAL 'EM.

THT!

THUD!

AH!

CRRRRR

SLAP!

HEY, CORY...

KEEP AN EYE ON YOUR BROTHER, WOULD YA?

CATCH YOU AROUND, GREY.

BUT... W--

WAIT.

FLOP!

SHOULD WE GO AFTER THEM?

VESPER?

VOLUME 3
COMING SOON

"It has been over four years since plume first hit the internet, over two years since it was brought to print, and now, Volume 2 is in your hands.

To those who supported the Kickstarter, you're amazing. The fact that you care enough about this project to put your hard-earned money behind it means the world to me. It is deeply humbling and extremely gratifying, and just a touch terrifying. I mean, really, you blew me away.

Here's to you, dear reader. Without your support, none of this would have been possible. **"**

— K. Lynn Smith

DEVIL'S DUE

plume
VOLUME TWO

Story & Art
by
K. Lynn Smith

Created
by
K. Lynn Smith

Edited
by
Josh Blaylock

Design & Production
by
Nick Accardi

For Devil's Due Ent.

Founder/Managing Principal: **Josh Blaylock**
Publishing Coordinator: **Kit Caoagas**
Lead Designer: **Nick Accardi**
Marketing/Crowdfunding Coordinator: **K. Lynn Smith**
Accounting: **Debbie Davis**
Media Contact: **Press@devilsdue.net**

www.DevilsDue.net